BIBLE FORTRESSES, TEMPLES &TOMBS

2:52

smarter • bigger • deeper • cooler

BIBLE FORTRESSES, TEMPLES & TOMBS

WRITTEN BY
RICK **OSBORNE**
MARNIE **WOODING**
ED **STRAUSS**

ILLUSTRATED BY
JACK **SNIDER**

Zonder**kidz**

Zonder**kidz**™

The children's group of Zondervan

www.zonderkidz.com

Editor: Gwen Ellis
Art direction & Interior design: Michelle Lenger

Printed in USA

03 04 05/RRD/5 4 3 2 1

CONTENTS

INTRODUCTION 6

1. NIMROD AND HIS AMAZING TOWER—BABEL 9
2. UR OF THE CHALDEANS 12
3. DAMASCUS—FULL OF HISTORY 17
4. EGYPT—HIGH-ENERGY BUILDERS 21
5. WORSHIPING ON THE RUN 31
6. LOST CITY OF PETRA 33
7. THE FIVE PHILISTINE CITIES 39
8. THE GREAT CITY OF JERUSALEM 45
9. SOLOMON'S JERUSALEM 49
10. JERUSALEM—A CITY UNDER ATTACK! 55
11. REBUILDING JERUSALEM 61
12. MIGHTY NINEVEH 67
13. BABYLON—QUEEN OF CITIES 71
14. BETHLEHEM—STARTING POINT 77
15. NAZARETH—JESUS' HOMETOWN 81
16. CAESAREA—CONCRETE PORT CITY 85
17. THE MASADA FORTRESS 89
18. CORINTH 93
19. ATHENS 97
20. ALEXANDRIA—IS GREAT! 101
21. EPHESUS 105
22. THE CITY OF ROME 109
23. LABYRINTH OF THE DEAD 117
24. NEW JERUSALEM—WHOLE NEW PLACE 121
CONCLUSION 125

INTRODUCTION

People have been building stuff ever since Adam and Eve left the Garden of Eden and had to find a place to live. No kidding! They probably built the first house on the planet. Now, no matter where we go on earth—the jungles of the Amazon to the tundra of the Arctic and everywhere in between—there are buildings. So how exactly did we get from huts to skyscrapers?

The Bible is filled with stories about amazing people, about the totally mysterious places where they lived, and the awesome buildings they built. So let's do some time-travel into the past to uncover hidden secrets of ancient master builders. We'll explore the pyramid tombs of powerful Egyptian pharaohs. We'll crawl through slimy water tunnels in Jerusalem. And we'll break into the most impenetrable fortresses ever built on this planet. When we investigate the ruins of Bible times, we are walking in the dusty footsteps of the heroes and bad guys of the past. Who knows what (or whom) we'll dig up?

NIMROD AND HIS AMAZING TOWER—BABEL

GENESIS 11:1—9

Hundreds of years after Noah and the Flood, the world's first megalomaniac ("I'm the greatest!"),Nimrod, began building cities all over the land of Mesopotamia. That's where the country of Iraq is today. He wanted to build an empire for himself. It would be known as (ta-da!) "the land of Nimrod."

Nimrod decided to build a tower so tall that it would reach heaven. The Bible tells us that loser Nimrod's tower of power—the Tower of Babel—was made of bricks. Brick-makers mixed together dirt, animal dung (you know, poop), and chopped-up straw to make strong, mud bricks. So plop, plop, chop, chop, mix, shape, and dry. They used tar to stick the bricks together. Tar is crude oil that seeps up from the earth and makes a smelly, oozing black pool. Pretty disgusting stuff! But it is great for sticking things together and for waterproofing boats and baskets.

God let them get started, and then he canceled Nimrod's building permit, his tower, and his total ego-head empire. God turned Nimrod's building site into a no-building zone.

ANCIENT BUILDING FACTS

- An ancient brick maker could make 3,000 sun-dried bricks a day.

- Ziggurats were the first skyscrapers. The Tower of Babel was probably a ziggurat. The word *ziggurat* means "mountain peak."

- Ziggurats were brick platforms stacked on top of each other—each stack smaller than the one below it—to make a tower.

- Archaeologists have found more than 25 of these ziggurat super towers!

- People called "Sumerians" built the ziggurats around 4,000 years ago.

- Researchers figure some ziggurats were 70 feet tall! (Very

impressive, considering the plop-chop they're built of, but hardly "up to heaven," huh, Nimrod?)
- When archaeologists went hunting for Nimrod's Tower of Babel, all they found was more dirt! All those bricks had disintegrated.

Ziggurats were built to impress the gods and to show off a king's wealth—an ancient way of saying, "Hey, look at me! I'm bigger and badder than you!" or maybe, "I can stack dung higher than you can!" And God's not going to put up with that kind of pride.

GET STRONGER

God didn't put a "stop work" order on the Tower of Babel to keep people from accomplishing big things. He put a stop to the project because Nimrod was going against God with his desire to build his tower to heaven. God wants us to do great things, but he wants us to do them with his direction and help. And God hates pride.

UR OF THE CHALDEANS

Let's check out the ancient riverside city of Ur. Ur was once the home of Abraham. It was a "lost city" for thousands of years. In fact, some people didn't think there had ever been a place named Ur.

Then Sir Charles Woolley started digging. And look what he found: A whole city—the city of Ur! Now look at those skeptics' red faces! Woolley found that Ur was huge—well, not huge by the kinds of cities we have today, but huge for then. It was two miles long by half a mile wide, with city walls a whopping 70 feet thick and 80 feet high. For ancient invaders to reach the top of the wall, they'd have had to stack 15 guys on each other's shoulders. Better get some ladders there, fellas!

Woolley also found 1,800 ancient burials or, as he liked to call them, "death pits" with bodies still in them! Nice find, Charlie—shriveled-up dead guys thousands of years old. Some of them were ancient kings and queens. But at this point that didn't make them any better looking! Gross out! One king's tomb contained the bodies of 59 servants who had been sacrificed. They were all lying in a neat line. They'd been poisoned so they could join their king in death. Now, you talk about "follow the leader!"

QUEEN OF THE DEAD

Sir Charles hit pay dirt at Ur when he discovered Queen Pu-Abi's small but extremely crowded burial pit. Here's a list of stuff the queen couldn't do without—and had buried with her.

- A fortune of gold and silver objects. Even gold drinking tubes (straws) and gold tools.
- Furniture, of course.
- Two dead oxen hooked up to a sled. Okaaay . . . that was a surprise.
- Four dead grooms to look after the dead oxen. Makes sense.

- Twelve dead slave girls. The body of one slave girl still had her fingers wrapped around the strings of her harp.
- Dead guards lying nearby. They had daggers to protect the queen. Somebody should have let the guards know she was already dead! But then, so were they.

It just doesn't get any creepier than that! It's no wonder God told Abraham to leave Ur.

GET DEEPER

These misguided Urites were wrong. They thought that by loading up their tombs with stuff and people, they'd have them in the after-life. (Can you say, "In error in Ur" ten times really fast?) Truth is, there's only one way to bring people with you into heaven, and that's by helping them accept Christ. You do that best by what you say and how you live.

DAMASCUS— FULL OF HISTORY

When it comes to old cities that are still around today, you really can't beat Damascus. People have been calling that particular city "home sweet home" for almost 6,000 years. (Today, over 1.4 million people live in Damascus.) So why has Damascus continued to be such a hot spot all these thousands of years? Well, it was a transportation hub—the super mall of the ancient world. Caravans of camels and donkeys weighed down with figs, wines, silks, gold, and silver plodded in and out of Damascus.

SOME NEAT CARAVAN FACTS

- Ancient caravans may have had 500 to 1,000 camels and donkeys. That's a lot of dung and puddles left behind in the streets.
- Camels can go two weeks without water.
- Camels can carry 1,000 pounds of goods.
- Arabian riding camels can travel 100 miles a day.

DAMASCUS UP FOR GRABS!

The metalsmiths of Damascus were known as the master sword makers of the world. The downside of all this wealth and success was that the city was a target for every passing army. So the city dwellers built defensive walls, forts, moats, and even trenches! Didn't help. An entire parade of empires and kings took over the city.

Some of those short-term city holders were: Arabs, Egyptians, Assyrians, Babylonians, Persians, Greeks, Romans, the Ottomans, the French, the Germans, the British, and the Turks. Even Goliath-killing King David once captured the city. And so did Alexander the Great, and a little while after him Pompey the Great (that's Pompey, not Popeye). During World War II the Germans took Damascus. A map of Damascus probably included not only tourist sites but also signs for which streets to use if you were a conquering army!

Other very famous people in the Bible visited Damascus, too: Abraham and Jacob passed by. When the apostle Paul tried to preach the gospel in Damascus, he had to escape the city by being lowered down the city wall in a basket (2 Corinthians 11:32–33). Some people thought that John the Baptist was the city's "head" guest. Legend has it that John's head was kept there after it had been chopped off by King Herod (Mark 6:26–28). Don't want to know what else people kept in their closets!

GET SMARTER

Easy come, easy go. Armies would win Damascus in a battle and then lose it the same way. Win—lose, win—lose. What if you desperately want something? How do you go about getting it? Taking it from another by force? Begging? The best way to get something is to trust God for it, because what you take from others can be taken from you. But what God gives you in his own time is more likely to last.

EGYPT— HIGH-ENERGY BUILDERS

By the time Joseph was taken to Egypt in chains (Genesis 37:28), the pyramids were already thousands of years old. Egypt started building pyramids and other monuments and buildings when people first began to settle in the Nile Valley. Over time, they built a powerful kingdom that stretched along 750 miles of the Nile River.

FACTS ABOUT EGYPT

- Egypt is thousands of years old.
- It was a powerful world kingdom for more than 2,000 years.
- Egypt's chariot-driven armies conquered many of the neighboring kingdoms and lands.
- It was totally rich and totally feared!

PYRAMIDS

Say the word *Egypt* and everybody thinks, "Oh yeah! Pyramids!" The Egyptian pyramids have to be some of the most famous piles of stone in the world. For about 4,000 years the ancient Egyptians really got into constructing pyramids.

Pyramids were built as tombs for the Egyptians' powerful kings, also known as *pharaohs*. The largest pyramid belonged to the mighty Pharaoh Khufu. It still stands today and it is 450 feet tall. When a king like Khufu came to power, he had to start building his pyramid tomb right away to get it finished by the time he died. It took a long time to build a pyramid.

There are more than two million limestone blocks in the pyramid of Khufu.

Each stone block weighs between 4,000 and 30,000 pounds! That's a lot of heavy rock.

It took teams of 4,000 workers about 23 years to build Khufu's pyramid. By comparison, it took around 3,000 workers one year (and seven million man-hours) to build the Empire State Building. But they had heavy-duty machine power doing the heavy stuff!

Researchers think the Egyptians constructed huge dirt ramps around the pyramid. Then teams of 18 to 20 guys dragged the stone blocks up the ramp and fitted them into place. Archaeologists have even found ancient stone workers' instructions on the blocks. Basically, notes like "This end up!" But ancient jokers who worked on the pyramids also wrote graffiti like, "How drunk is the king!"

Inside Khufu's pyramid is an eerie series of dark hallways, air shafts, and chambers. The king's burial chamber has six huge granite roof-stones to keep the

weight of the pyramid from caving in on the tomb. Kings could also be a pain! It seems King Khufu had twice ordered his burial chamber enlarged and moved higher up in the pyramid. He must have driven his architect crazy! ("If the king calls, don't answer.")

HIDDEN IN THE SANDS OF TIME

Everybody knows about the very cool Sphinx of Egypt. You know, the funny-looking stone guy hanging around the pyramids with a human head and a lion's body, but the poor dude's missing his nose and beard!

- The Sphinx is 240 feet long and 66 feet tall. (That's six feet taller than the four presidential faces on Mount Rushmore.)
- Today the Sphinx's very cool goatee can be found on display in the British Museum.

- His nose? The rumor is that around 1799, Napoleon Bonaparte's French troops used the Sphinx's nose for target practice and shot it off. No one really "nose."
- The ancient Greeks were the first to call him "Sphinx"—after a creepy half-beast and half-human monster from their own legends.
- The Sphinx is thought to be 4,500 years old—or maybe older!
- Looks as if ancient repair guys fixed the paws at least three times.
- The Sphinx may have been built as a guardian to protect the royal tombs. It is built of very soft sandstone. So the fact that sand had piled-up around the Sphinx, probably helped preserve him.

Researchers figure that if workers stopped clearing away the sand right now, in 20 years the Sphinx would be completely covered up again.

So what's the full scoop on this noseless, beardless, part-lion guy? Why was he built? How long ago? What for? No one really knows. Hey, maybe the answers are still buried in the sand.

RAMSES' CITY—PI-RAMSES

Like most pharaohs, Ramses II liked to do things in a very big way. He fought big battles, had a big family (100 kids), and built really outrageously extravagant temples. He had two very large temples carved into the sandstone cliffs along the upper Nile. Guarding the entrance of the largest temple are four six-foot-tall statues of (who else?) himself. What an ego-head!

This is probably the pharaoh who totally gave Moses a hard time. Researchers have put out a long list of Egyptian kings who might have been the pharaoh who oppressed the Hebrews. They don't agree on which one it was, but a good guess is that it was Ramses II. We find lots of ancient bricks with R2's name stamped on them. And the Bible tells us the Hebrews spent a ton of time making a ton of royal bricks (Exodus 1:14). Hey, the "fun" just never ended in old Egypt. Yuck to being a slave!

Now, Ramses had a big port city built called Pi-Ramses, complete with palace, barracks, and store-houses. But nobody can find any record of Egyptians working on the city. So-o-o . . . you have to wonder if maybe the builders were all Hebrew slaves? We know that they *did* build a city called Ramses, after all (Exodus 1:11).

Modern archaeologists, using a totally cool system called magnetic photography, were able to take pictures of this huge, 3,000-year-old city while it is still buried under farmers' fields. What they saw gave them the complete picture about the city hidden below their feet:

- It was 240-acre city complete with houses, streets, and palaces. Have you ever been to Disneyland in California? Well, Ramses was bigger than that.
- It had one of the largest stables in the ancient world, which would have held hundreds of horses. (Anyone want a job cleaning stables?)
- It had workshops that made chariots and weapons.
- And of course, what ancient city would be complete without a few temples?

TREASURE QUEST

The Valley of the Kings is the ancient burial ground of some of the greatest pharaohs of Egypt. In 1916 a man, Howard Carter, was convinced that the tomb of a young king named Tutankhamen was buried somewhere in the valley. But where? It was truly a hide-and-seek game. To protect their treasure, pharaohs built their tombs secretly, had false passages made to throw off burglars, and even dumped rubble at the entrances to hide their tombs and treasure.

So, how do you find something that someone has tried very, very hard to hide? Simple—dig *everywhere* in the valley for six lo-o-ong years. And then, when you have dug everywhere, you order your crew to dig once more beneath the ruins of huts used by ancient workers. On November 4, 1922, Carter's diggers discovered a stairway leading deep into the earth. Howard had twice been within a few feet of discovering the entrance! That is a total bummer.

After struggling through one sealed door and an inner hallway full of rubble, Howard finally found a door that had King Tut's royal symbol on it. *Now* he was getting somewhere! He drilled a hole in the door and sent the first ray of light into the tomb in 3,000 years. What did he see? "Strange animals, statues, and gold—everywhere gold," he said. This tomb was the only one in the valley that had survived thousands of years of being searched by grave robbers. Even those who built the ancient tombs used to go back and rob the pharaohs.

SOME OF THE TOMB'S TREASURES:

• A solid-gold, 242-pound coffin (Equal to ten 27-pound bars of gold.) The gold in the coffin alone is worth several million dollars.

- A golden death mask
- A six-foot-long wooden lion covered in gold
- A royal, golden dagger
- A throne of gold and semiprecious stones

Tutankhamen was only 19 when he died and wasn't very famous back then. But now in death he's one of the world's most famous superstar pharaohs!

GET SMARTER

The pharaohs spent a lot of time and money building stone monuments to themselves and their great king-li-ness. Yet today about all we know about them or their greatness is that they knew how to build big buildings. Compare that with Moses, who probably never built a building but spent his time obeying God and helping others. Pharaohs are forgotten, but Moses is remembered. It's more important to build great character than to build great monuments.

WORSHIPING ON THE RUN

After the Hebrews left Egypt, they spent 40 years trudging through the dusty desert. Just think of it: Forty years of sand, dust, sunburn, and being sandblasted when the wind blew. But God was with them. He wanted them to have a place to worship on the go. Dragging a stone temple with them was totally out of the question. So God gave Moses a design for the first-ever mobile temple—a holy tent! The tent and its contents were made of valuable skins, cloth, jewels, and gold and were put together by the best, most skilled craftsmen. What they made were works of art kept in the most beautiful and expensive tent ever made! (See Exodus 26.)

The most wonderful object inside this holy tent was a gorgeous golden chest—the ark of the covenant (Exodus 25:10–22). If there was one thing that gave the enemies of Israel the willies, the ark was it. When the Israelites won battle after battle against incredible odds, word got out that their God was fighting for them. The ark was a symbol of God's power and presence.

About the Tabernacle

- It was set up right in the center of camp.
- A seven-and-a-half-foot-tall curtain closed off a 150-foot-long by 75-foot-wide courtyard.
- The tabernacle and its courtyard fences were staked out using miles of rope.
- The tent was a "priest only" tent and was divided into two rooms—the outer and inner rooms.

- Only the high priest could enter the inner-most holy room, and then only on one special day each year. When he went into the holiest room, he had a rope tied around his ankle in case he made God angry and God killed him! If that happened, others could drag him out by the rope.

- Inside the holiest room was the ark of the covenant. Inside the ark, the Israelites kept the Ten

Commandments, a pot of manna, and Aaron's rod—the one that bloomed, got leaves, and even had almonds grow on it even though it wasn't connected to a tree.

- The ark was as large as a very big sea trunk or pirate's treasure chest.

It was the most important possession the Israelites had. One day it simply vanished from history. There are theories that it may still be around somewhere today, but no one knows for sure—at least no one who's talking.

GET DEEPER

The Israelites were in awe of the ark and the holy tent because they knew that God's presence and power were in them. The New Testament tells us that Christians are the temple of God's Spirit (1 Corinthians 3:16). So the same awesome presence and power of God that was in the ark, is in us and with us. What an awesome truth!

LOST CITY OF PETRA

In 1812, a daring Swiss explorer and archaeologist named Johann Burckhardt disguised himself as a Muslim trader and convinced an Arab guide to take him to a mysterious lost city. His guide led him through a mile-long, twisting sandstone ravine, deeper and deeper into the mountains. What Johann found when he finally stepped into the hidden valley, stunned him. He had found an ancient lost city! Beautiful buildings were carved into the pink sandstone of the valley's 250-foot-high walls. For 300 years people had told stories about the legendary lost city of Petra. Now, Johann was standing there.

Petra was inhabited for thousands of years during a good portion of biblical history. Some people think that the apostle Paul visited Petra during the two years that he was hiding out in Arabia (Galatians 1:17).

Ancient Arabs (called Nabataeans) dug and carved a city right out of the sandstone cliffs. Caravans carrying frankincense, myrrh, silks from China, jewels from India, figs from Israel, and spices from Asia, stopped and rested at Petra, for a price, of course. This made Petra stinking rich!

The Nabataeans built expensive tombs, temples, and even a theater that could seat 3,000 people. They cut stairs all the way up the ravine to a great rock hundreds of feet above. Here, on top, they chipped away the stone until two 20-foot-high pillars stood in the spot. (The valley walls of Petra, at 250 feet high, would tower over Niagara Falls, which is only 182 feet tall.)

What happened to Petra? How did it get lost? Times change and so do caravan routes and empires. Researchers think that another city, called Palmyra, eventually took away most of Petra's business, and the city died. A few people were probably still living there during the Crusades in the Middle Ages, but the great city of Petra was soon left to the desert sands.

Archaeologists have found coins, pottery, papyrus manuscripts, oil lamps, and even Egyptian-style bronze statues in the city, showing that people from many lands passed that way.

GET DEEPER

The inhabitants of Petra carved phenomenal, rich, spacious dwellings out of the rose-colored rock. Builders of such big places often assume that having more-splendid surroundings means a greater life. But without God and his peace, all big places do is make it harder for you to find the bathroom at night.

THE FIVE PHILISTINE CITIES

The Philistines had five, large, city kingdoms, but it seems no Philistine town had as much of an in-your-face reputation as good ol' Gath. It was the hometown of that nine-foot-tall monster warrior Goliath and his equally large brothers. Gath was mega-fortified, just like many other Philistine cities, and had huge, heavy city gates.

There are archaeologists who believe they have found the city of Gath on top of a 695-foot-tall hill. Perfect location! Always make your attackers sweat buckets trying to climb up to your city. Gath must have had a strong city wall to keep out attackers, but being on top of a big hill and having a big wall didn't always keep cities safe. At Gath, archaeologists found a huge, man-made, dry moat—25 feet wide and 13 feet deep—around the city. It had been dug by an attacking army to keep the people of Gath trapped inside. This moat meant:

• No sneaking out to attack the sleeping siege camp

- No sneaking in food or messages
- Absolutely no leaving in fast war-chariots

Clearly, this moat had Gath trapped. The attacking soldiers even piled the dirt from the moat on the city side to protect themselves from Gath's arrows and spears. It took a lot of work to make this moat deep and wide. That meant that the city was probably under attack for a long time. The Bible tells us that Gath was destroyed by the mighty King Hazael of Aram (2 Kings 12:17). Was this moat his handiwork? Might have been. Every bully eventually meets a bigger bully, and the bully Philistines finally met their match.

TEMPLES OF THE PHILISTINES

Muscle-man Samson (Philistine public enemy number one) pushed on two temple pillars with all his strength until they cracked, crashing the crumbling roof on the craniums of the crowd (Judges 16:25–30). Three thousand Philistines were squashed like bugs. Including Samson. Which reminds us—when push comes to shove, even good guys can get hurt.

So have our archaeological super sleuths ever found the ruins of the Philistine's demolished temple? Well, when digging at a place called Tell Qasile, they found a Philistine mud-brick temple with two, large, support pillars set only six feet apart. Hmmm, that's within pushing distance. Only problem is, the Bible tells us that the Philistines took Samson to the city of Gaza, which was 65 miles down the coast from this temple (Judges 16:21). Right idea . . . wrong temple. But

were other Philistine temples built the same way, with support pillars set close together? Yes, at place called Beth-Shean. So there could also be a Samson-like temple buried in Gaza, just waiting to be discovered.

ASHDOD AND THE ARK

The Philistines worshiped a fishy-looking fish god by the name of Dagon. They even had images of this sucker on their coins. The Philistines believed that this fish god helped them win their battles. *Not likely.* But once when the Israelites were disobeying God, God let the Philistines capture the ark of the covenant. This was a really big deal because the Philistines knew that stealing the ark would really freak out the Israelites.

To thank their god, Dagon, for this victory, the Philistines took the ark to his temple in the powerful city of Ashdod. They set the ark of God right in front of their idol of Dagon. What happened next had all of Ashdod freaked! In the morning they found their fish god flat on his nose—as if he'd fallen down to worship God. They propped Mr. Fish God up again, buuut . . . the next day he'd belly-flopped again and was a headless, handless, fallen loser.

Soon all the people of the city were running around with painful lumps growing on them. Oh, great! Now the ark's brought us a plague! Maybe someone else would like to "enjoy" it for a while? They packed it up and sent it to the Philistine town of Gath. The plague hit Gath too. Whoa! Let's mark that Israelite ark: "Return to sender" and get it out of here. They begged the Israelites to take it back. (Check out this very cool story in 1 Samuel 4–6.)

GET STRONGER

Here come the big Philistines in their big boats, building their big cities and big temples, with their big, giant warriors. But God put them in their place. He used one very angry strongman, one shepherd boy with a sling, and one small, stolen, gold-covered box. It does not matter if you are small; it's who's on your side that counts.

THE GREAT CITY OF JERUSALEM

Jerusalem began as a tough, little, hilltop fortress called Jebus. King David decided to make Jebus his new capital. The Jebusites weren't going along with his plan. They liked their city just the way it was—without Israelites! So, when King David came by, they leaned over the walls, hooting and mocking him and saying that he could never capture their city.

David didn't like being laughed at very much, but what could he do? Jebus was built on the highest plateau in all of Canaan and was surrounded by rugged valleys. This made the city impossible to attack from the west, south, or east. And the north wasn't easy, either. That's exactly the reason why David wanted the city—it was so well-protected by the land around it. But how to get it?

The entire city watched David and his soldiers. The Jebusites were having a party! They teased David's men, saying that even their grandmothers could defend the city against David's men. David's band of men hiked around the city, looking for a way to get in and found it!

Now it was payback time. David had his men climb up a secret under-ground water shaft that led right up into the city. Of course, they took the city and—sur-prise, surprise!—David got his new capital and named it Jerusalem (2 Samuel 5:6–7).

Over thousands of years, the shaft that gave David his victory was forgotten, but in 1867 a British officer named Charles Warren was exploring the tunnels under Jerusalem when his team discovered a 52-foot-long shaft cut into the rock under the city. In ancient times when there was war, the inhabitants of Jerusalem would travel through secret tunnels to the shaft and then lower buckets down to pull up water from the Gihon spring below. Warren wondered if he had rediscovered David's secret water shaft. Could this vertical tunnel actually be climbed? British army officers in 1910 managed to climb the shaft, but it wasn't easy, even with climbing equipment. So could it have been possible for David's men to climb it, thousands of years earlier? Hey! It's amazing what guys will do when they're being mocked and want to get even with the mockers. Most researchers agree that David's men did climb that shaft. But it would be like climbing a dark, wet, slippery, broken, twisted, five-story elevator shaft.

GET COOLER

It's easy to be nice to people when we think we have something to gain by being nice. It's also easy to be nasty to people when we think we have nothing to lose. The Jebusites were mean and made fun of David because they thought they had nothing to lose. But they learned otherwise. They lost everything. We should be nice to everyone, win or lose. It's the right thing to do, and you never know who might be winning tomorrow.

SOLOMON'S JERUSALEM

King David left his kingdom and his capital city to his son Solomon. Soon King Solomon had merchant ships sailing all over the ancient seas. He had fabulous gold mines and a big business buying and selling Egyptian horses and chariots. The guy was a major mover and shaker. History tells us that silver, gold, and precious stones were common everywhere in Solomon's kingdom. Naturally, a king like that needed a big and important-looking city. So Solomon began to renovate the little fortress town of Jerusalem. After 13 years of building, Jerusalem had expanded north from the original city of Jebus to include the temple mountain, Solomon's palace, and all the other buildings that kept his government and palace running. Solomon's city was now spread over 20 to 35 acres of land.

How Solomon Built a Royal City

- He gathered many taxes from the 12 tribes of Israel.
- He forced every man in his kingdom to work four months of the year for the king. (Thirty thousand guys would be working for the king at any, one, time.)
- He made captured, foreign soldiers and citizens build for him for free. (Ummm, isn't that slavery?)
- In Jerusalem Solomon's workforce built God's temple, Solomon's palace, a new city wall, a huge fort, an entire city for his horses and chariots, a palace for a wife who just happened to be an Egyptian princess, and a huge storage city. In fact, Solomon's palace and other government buildings doubled the amount of land used by the royal court.

Solomon's Temple

It took Solomon seven years to build a temple to God in Jerusalem (1 Kings 6:37–38). By today's standards it wasn't giganto-normous. It was only 93 feet long, 45 feet wide, and about three stories high—as tall as the White House in Washington, D.C. The temple had an outer space for worship and sacrifice, a large outer room, and an inner holy chamber where the ark was kept. So why'd it take so long to build?

First, it was the quietest construction site in history! No building noise was allowed in the temple area. No hammers, axes, or any metal tools could be used, because of the noise they made (1 Kings 6:7).

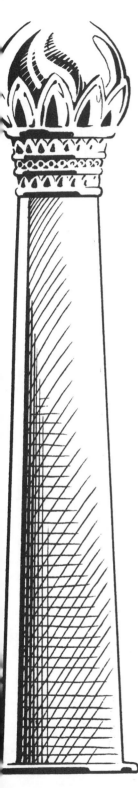
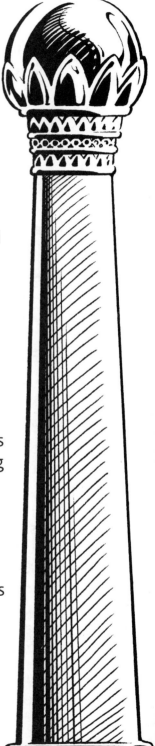

All the timber, stone blocks, and other materials had to be cut and shaped far away and then quietly brought to the site and fitted together.

Only the very best materials would do! Gold, silver, precious stones, expensive cloth, and the best woods of cedar, cypress, and olive were all brought to Jerusalem (1 Kings 5–7).

The inside walls of the temple were plastered with gold. Sol even used gold nails weighing 20 ounces each! That's a lot of gold. But no problemo! Solomon was raking in over 50,000 pounds of gold a year (1 Kings 10:14). That's billions of dollars' worth! This king was loaded! When the temple was finally built, Solomon sacrificed 22,000 oxen and 120,000 sheep and goats to honor God (1 Kings 8:62–63). Put on rubber boots because that's mega-gallons of blood flowing from the altar!

Solomon's temple is gone now. For hundreds of years either different kings stripped the gold off the temple for their own purposes, or invading kings robbed the city and stole the temple gold. According to Egyptian records, Pharaoh Shishak stole about 200 tons of gold from Jerusalem (see 2 Chronicles 12:9). God allowed this because his people were disobedient and it took drastic deeds to get their attention.

After each raid, the good kings of Israel did their best to fix and restore the temple to its original glory. Finally, at a point when the Jewish people were being really disobedient, God allowed a big, bad Babylonian king named Nebuchadnezzar to completely destroy it (2 Chronicles 36:15–19). But that still wasn't the end of God's house in Jerusalem.

READINESS AND FORTS

In Solomon's day, Jerusalem was one of the richest cities in the world because Israel was a vast empire, from Egypt in the south to the Euphrates River in the north. When you're that rich and that powerful, you have to expect that bullies will want a piece of your action. Solomon decided to give his huge workforce the job of building walls or repairing and building new forts around his kingdom. Smart move. To handle all the building that Solomon wanted done, he had 80,000 stonecutters, 70,000 guys to carry supplies and materials, and 3,300 supervisors—and they were just part of his building crews (1 Kings 5:15–16). In more modern history, it took ten years for 75,000 workers to build the 50-mile-long Panama Canal.

Solomon couldn't afford to build forts everywhere, so he selected only the most important sites around the country. From those forts his soldiers could quickly move out and stop invading armies in their tracks.

King David's army was mostly made up of foot soldiers, but his son Sol added soldiers on horseback and in chariots. He wanted his army to have speed on their side. He had 12,000 men and 1,400 chariots on shift duty day or night. When his fortresses were completed, Solomon could stop invasions from the sea, the plains, valley passes, and main roads. His forts also protected important trade routes into his kingdom, and Israel's borders, from the almost constant raiding by desperate desert people. All of Solomon's forts seemed to have been built the same way, with thick outer and inner protective walls, storerooms, barracks, and six-chambered gates in the walls.

GET STRONGER

It's always been cool to be really rich. Solomon would fit right in with today's rich celebrities. But Sol, just like modern people, found out that being rich and doing things big didn't make him happy. Sometimes it just brought him trouble and a lot of work and worry. Happiness and peace don't come from more things. They come from God.

JERUSALEM — A CITY UNDER ATTACK!

After Solomon died, his mighty kingdom was split into two smaller kingdoms, Israel and Judah (1 Kings 11:34–37). If that weren't bad enough, new super-bullies called the Assyrians were in town.

After years and years of being pushed around by the Assyrians, a good king named Hezekiah decided to break Judah free. He prepared Jerusalem for a long siege by repairing the walls and making a ton of weapons. He also ordered the city's water source (the Gihon spring, outside the city walls) to be sealed off and channeled by secret tunnel into the city (2 Chronicles 32:30; 2 Kings 20:20). Two teams of workers were put on the job. Ancient writing (probably a worker's) scratched in the wall of the tunnel, tells us the story:

One team of diggers started inside the city, and another started down at the Gihon spring.

Both teams dug into the rock under the city, with the idea of meeting somewhere in the

middle. But . . . The diggers didn't dig in a straight
line! They curved around, probably following underground streams and breaks in the stone. They nearly
missed each other! Fortunately, they heard the other
crew's pickaxes and dug toward the noise. The S-
shaped water tunnel is an impressive 1,750 feet long.

Tunnel building hasn't changed that much since
Hezekiah's time—start at the ends and meet in the
middle. But the size of the tunnel has gotten just a little bigger. Recently an amazing army of 13,000 workers dug out a whopping 95 miles of rock to build the
underwater Channel Tunnel that connects Great
Britain and Europe.

In 1838 an American explorer, Edward Robinson, took
a team of men through Hezekiah's tunnel, from one
end to the other. The tunnel was 20 feet high in some
sections while, in other spots, the men had to crawl
through on their stomachs. Today, 2,500 years after it
was built, the tunnel still brings water to the Pool of

Siloam inside the city. And did the Assyrians whip
Hezekiah? Nope! God sent an angel to kill 185,000 of
their soldiers camped outside the city (2 Kings 19:35).

BABYLONIAN THUGS

News flash: Assyrians get smashed by an even
stronger Babylonian empire. The leader of the
Babylonians was a tough-talking, bone-crushing king
named Nebuchadnezzar. And he warned Judah, "No
funny business! Behave or else!"

But sneaky Egypt kept pressuring the kings of Judah
to rebel against Nebuchadnezzar. The last straw was
when Judah's King Zedekiah joined with Egypt to fight
Nebuchadnezzar. This made the Babylonian big guy
really, really mad. He took his army and surrounded
Jerusalem for 18 months. On the night the
Babylonians broke through the walls, creepy King
Zedekiah and his army fled the city—leaving his starv-
ing people to face the music.

- Nebuchadnezzar completely torched and destroyed Jerusalem.
- He captured almost all the people and shipped them back to Babylonia.
- He demolished Solomon's temple, taking all the silver and gold from inside—oh yeah, and don't forget those 27-foot bronze pillars out front.

- King Zedekiah was caught, had his eyes poked out, and was held in Neb's prison for life (2 Kings 25:1–15).

We know a lot about this time in history, but what we don't know is: What happened to the ark of the covenant? Did the Babylonians take it? Or is it hidden in a secret cave somewhere under Jerusalem? Nobody knows. That's an unsolved mystery.

GET DEEPER

Is this like a pattern or what? When the Israelites trusted and obeyed God, things went well for them. When they didn't, life began to stink. Of course, it took a while to get to the stink level. They'd fall away from God slowly over the years. For a while things would be good—then *bam!* Life with God is still like that. It doesn't become all good or all bad all of a sudden. Want good to happen? Keep on trusting and obeying God and he'll reward you (Hebrews 11:6).

REBUILDING JERUSALEM

King David's great city of Jerusalem lay in ruins after its people were taken to Babylonia by his royal badness, Nebuchadnezzar. God had said that they'd be gone from their land for 70 years, and sure enough, they were. Then a new and powerful empire—the Persians— crunched the Babylonians. But, hey, King Cyrus, the Persian king, let the Israelites return to their homeland and rebuild God's temple. He even let them take back the temple gold that the Babylonians had ripped off (Ezra 1).

The Jewish people rebuilt the temple, but we really don't know that much about its size or dimensions. The Bible says that their new neighbors dis- couraged them. So, it took them 15 years to rebuild it. Researchers figure it must have looked similar to Solomon's temple but not nearly as flashy. It lasted 500 years anyway.

A later Persian king, Artaxerxes, put his own Israelite wine-taster, Nehemiah, in charge of rebuilding Jerusalem's walls. The Jewish people were happy, but the foreigners who now lived in the land were very unhappy, so Nehemiah's workers packed weapons to protect themselves while they built (Nehemiah 4:13–16).

JERUSALEM IN JESUS' DAY

In 20 B.C., about 15 years before Jesus was born, Jerusalem was once again a big, busy, important city. By then the dreaded Roman Empire had marched in and taken over the place. Nobody was happy about that! Well . . . except maybe the Israelite king, Herod the Great. (The Romans sort of let him play king.) But Herod was bad news. He loved to kill people! Like many totally evil megalomaniacs, however, he was into building impressive stuff—like a brand-new, awesome temple in Jerusalem.

If you weren't Jewish, you didn't need to expect a tour. The sign out front read, "No foreigner may pass the barrier and enclosure surrounding the temple. Anyone who is caught doing so will

have himself to blame for his resulting death."
It was written in Greek and Latin. Real inviting!

Herod really wanted to impress the Jews (and make them like him—which they didn't), so he made the temple grounds twice as big as before. The people were not impressed.

TEMPLE FACTS

- The temple area was now the size of 12 soccer fields.
- Some of the surrounding walls were 165 feet tall!

- The larger stone blocks were 64 feet long, 14 feet high, and 11 feet wide. That made them weigh a backbreaking 415 tons.
- Herod had 1,000 wagons working overtime on the project.
- While the entire temple complex took many years to complete, the temple itself was completed in under 10 years.
- One area had 162 stone columns that were 27 feet tall.
- The temple had huge courtyards, gates, watchtowers, stairways, and even 30 pools (baths).

Let's compare this temple with one of the most famous cathedrals in the world—Notre Dame in Paris. It is 110 feet tall, has huge stained-glass windows, 386 stairs, and sports a 13-ton bell. But it was started in 1163 and finished 87 years later! You could put [how many temples?] inside it. Hey, Herod only took ten years to build his temple! Maybe that's why they called him "Great". It sure wasn't because of his personality.

- They were still building the temple complex when Jesus was crucified.
- Herod's temple was completely destroyed by the Romans only six years after it was finished. (Like, was that wasted effort or what?)
- Only part of a lower outside wall—that was never part of the Temple itself—remains today. Jewish people refer to is as "The Western Wall."

GET DEEPER

These ancient builders of the temple thought they had a better plan than the one God gave them. God had given the original instructions for building Solomon's temple, including size. Herod thought that he had a better plan and he built his temple larger. Herod probably thought that God would overlook all his wicked behavior if he built a really great temple. Wrong, Herod! We please God by trusting him and doing things his way. If we don't, we're going in the wrong direction, no matter what we do to try to make up for it.

MIGHTY NINEVEH

A man named Paul Emile Botta wandered around Iraq looking at ancient bricks and puzzling at the strange writing on them. He was curious, so he ordered his team of diggers to start work on a *tell* (an old city mound) along the Tigris River. Just below the surface—clunk!—diggers hit pay dirt! Botta had found Nineveh, the royal city of the Assyrians—the bad boys who had kicked sand in the faces of the Philistines and Egyptians, and had won!

In its prime time, Nineveh had 120,000 people living in it (Jonah 4:11). That was a big city at the time. Today's winner of the "largest city in the world" award goes to Mexico City, with a big population of over 15,047,685 people!

NINEVEH POWER FACTS

- Foreign captives dragged through Nineveh were awed and terrified by what they saw.
- Nineveh was a huge city, covering more land than 1,000 football fields.
- Surrounding Nineveh, were more than seven miles of defensive walls.

- The city had 15 main gates guarded by huge stone winged-bull statues 16 feet tall. Some guardian statues weighed 30 to 40 tons. Each. That's about the weight of six elephants!
- Sennacherib held court in a huge 80-room palace called the Palace Without Rival—meaning no one had a better one.
- The city had stables, military storehouses, and huge areas for training soldiers.
- The king built an impressive royal road 90 feet wide! That's like an eight-lane superhighway.

Along the walls of the king's palace were spooky carvings of his war victories. One palace had two miles of stone carvings. Assyrians liked to show scenes such as captive kings begging for mercy. Or piles of enemies' cut-off heads. Talk about a "head count." No wonder that captive kings were begging for mercy.

Now picture God's gutsy prophet Jonah walking up and telling the entire city, including the king, "Get right with God! Now!" (Jonah 3).

Later, after they forgot what Jonah had said, another prophet, named Nahum, said that Nineveh was going to bite the dust big-time (book of Nahum). And it did! The Assyrians had conquered so much land that they couldn't control it. You know, biting off more than they could chew. Now the conquered people fought back and regained their lands. Finally, Nineveh was attacked by the Babylonians, set on fire, wiped out, its people killed or enslaved. Hey, not so tough now, are you, Assyrian bad boys?

GET SMARTER

When you get into trouble and bad stuff happens, it's easy to "learn your lesson" because it helps the trouble go away. The trick is to *remember* what you learned and keep following it even though the trouble isn't there anymore. Nineveh smartened up for a while after Jonah said they'd be destroyed, but as the years went by, they forgot the lesson. Then really big trouble came, and they didn't get a warning.

BABYLON— QUEEN OF CITIES

The Babylonians totally annihilated the Assyrians and then built an even bigger city, called Babylon. In 1899, a guy from Germany named Robert Koldewey started digging in the ruins of Babylon. This guy was an unstoppable digging machine. He kept it up for 18 lo-o-ong years. You name it, the guy dug it up: temples, palaces, houses, city walls, and even roads!

BIG BABYLON

- The Babylonian royal city had over 200,000 people living in it and covered 2,000 acres.
- The king built a royal roadway that was 66 feet wide—and had sidewalks.
- Nebuchadnezzar had not one but two palaces in the city! He chose to conduct business in his heavily guarded Southern Palace. Smart move.
- His throne room was large and impressive: 56 feet wide and 170 feet long.
- Nebuchadnezzar's throne room walls didn't have battle scenes. It had pretty animal and flower designs. But don't let the girlie stuff fool you: This king was one tough dude!

Babylonian Defenses

When it came to defending his royal city, the king of the Babylonians was a very serious guy. The first thing visitors saw when they approached the city was five miles of defensive wall. But wait, that was only the first wall! That's right, there was more than one! The city had layers of kill-o-matic defenses!

- A 150-foot-wide outer moat kept defenders stuck on the far shore.
- A 12-foot-thick outer wall boasted guard towers every 67 feet.
- Invaders had to crash through eight, huge, bronze, outer gates set along the outer wall. (Yeah, right. Just try kicking in a bronze gate!)

The inner defensive wall was actually made up of two, thick, brick walls built close together. One was 21 feet thick and the other was 12 feet thick. The 24-foot space between the walls was filled in with rubble to make a military road on top of the wall. This road was wide enough to allow a four-horse war-chariot to patrol from above.

- The city also had a 262-foot-wide inner moat.
- Ancient travelers reported that the walls were 320 feet tall.

One of the most impressive gates in Babylon was the 70-foot-high Ishtar Gate. The gate was decorated with 200 molded dragons and bulls set on blue tile. This gate still exists and can now be found in Berlin! But

50 years ago the government of Iraq made a model of the gate and put it at the entrance to their new museum. It's not the real thing, but it's close.

BABYLON'S HANGING GARDENS

The ancient Greeks tell us that King Nebuchadnezzar built a mountainlike garden beside his palace to please a homesick wife from the hills. Greek visitors talked of a man-made mountain made up of balconies full of plants, exotic animals, and waterfalls. They said this huge riverside garden was 80 feet high and 400 feet wide and deep. Sounds impressive but, once again, did it really exist?

In 1899, our nonstop digger friend Robert Koldewey found what many think could be the foundation of Neb's garden. It was half the size of what the Greek tourists had reported, but then, maybe ancient travelers exaggerated ju-u-ust a little.

Speaking of ancient travelers, the Greeks and Romans put out a travel guide of "must see" amazing structures called The Seven Wonders of the Ancient World. They are:

- The Hanging Gardens of Babylon
- The Pyramids of Egypt
- The 40-foot Statue of Zeus in the Temple of Zeus at Olympia, Greece
- The Temple of Artemis at Ephesus (more on that, later)
- The marble tomb of Halicarnassus in Turkey, a 140-foot-tall tomb built by an ancient queen for her dead husband (not that he was that big)
- The Colussus of Rhodes, a 100-foot bronze statue of the Greek sun god Helios, set at the entrance of the harbor of Rhodes, Greece
- The 440-foot-tall Lighthouse of Alexandria in Egypt (more on that later)

GET SMARTER

God raised up Nebuchadnezzar, Cyrus, and other kings. Even though they were not worshipers of God, he used them to do his will (Isaiah 44:28; Jeremiah 27:5–8). When we're willing to do big things for God, he'll use us. But if we then start thinking that we're special, watch out. Pride comes before a fall (Proverbs 16:18). Belshazzar was a great king, but he was prideful and thought he could do whatever he wanted. He found out that he could not (Daniel 5).

When King David was a kid, his hometown of Bethlehem was a quiet village in the hills. It overlooked an ancient caravan route. Back then, the village was taken over by iron-sword-swinging Philistines (1 Chronicles 11:16). When David became king, he and his mighty men sent them packing. One of his mighty men, named Abishai, used his spear and nothing more to kill 300 guys at once (1 Chronicles 11:20). He was a mighty man!

Later on, Bethlehem became an important stopping point for caravans on their way to Egypt. In fact, a *caravanserai*—sort of an ancient motel for traveling traders—was built there.

STAYING AT THE INN

A caravanserai was usually a big, stone motel fort. It had sleeping rooms for people, stalls for animals, and a large protected courtyard.

These "motels" were spaced along travel routes all over the ancient world.

During a census that Herod commanded where everyone had to return to his or her hometown, caravanserai would be completely filled. That's what happened when Mary and Joseph came looking for a place to stay in Bethlehem (Luke 2:1–7).

All around town, the hills were full of caves. Jesus was probably born in one of these caves. At the time of his birth, the cave was being used as an animal shelter. It most likely held a manger where the animals ate.

For hundreds of years, Christians have traveled to world-famous Bethlehem to see the "exact" spot where Jesus was born! The truth is, we may never know for sure if today's tourist attraction is really the right cave. It doesn't matter, because we know that the most famous of all births took place in Bethlehem one amazing night 2,000 years ago!

GET STRONGER

One of the most important events in all of history, the birth of the Messiah, took place in a very unimportant town—little old Bethlehem. In the same way, God often uses small and humble people to accomplish great things. He could use big people, but they are usually too busy for God. They're not available. And what God wants most is someone who is available.

Are you available?

NAZARETH— JESUS' HOMETOWN

Jesus was born in Bethlehem, but he grew up in a hill-town called Nazareth, located about 14 miles from the Sea of Galilee. Many Jews considered Nazareth a "hick" town. They thought people there were rude and stupid. A guy named Nathanael even said, "Nazareth! Can anything good come from there?" (John 1:46). What a rotten attitude! When Jesus began to travel to other parts of the Promised Land, people called him Jesus of Nazareth. If they thought he was rude and uneducated, boy, were they wrong (John 7:15). This guy from Nazareth was smart, smart, smart!

When Jesus was growing up in Nazareth, there might have been around 15,000 people living there. He probably worked in the carpenter shop and helped Joseph make things such as furniture, baskets, and ceiling beams for houses.

A few miles away was the big city of Sepphoris, which also happened to be the Roman capital of Galilee. Perhaps at times Jesus and Joseph may have found work in the bigger city. Researchers figure that there were at least 30,000 people living there, and a real mix of people, too—Jews, Arabs, Greeks and, of course, Romans.

SEPPHORIS

- The city was on top of a 400-foot-high hill.
- It had an amphitheater, dug into the side of the hill that seated 4,500 people. The stage was 156 feet wide and 27 feet deep.
- The limestone-cobbled streets were in use for 500 years.
- The streets show deep ruts from wagons rolling over the same spots for hundreds of years.
- The city even had covered sidewalks.

Jesus would have made trips to Sepphoris and learned what a big city was like.

GET DEEPER

Jesus said that a prophet is never accepted in his own hometown, and he wasn't (Mark 6:4). People in Nazareth just blew him off as the "carpenter's kid." Many kids today believe that one has to be "born special," or born in a special place or to special parents, in order to be somebody. But God has a wonderful plan for each of our lives. It doesn't matter what "nowhere" town you come from. All you have to do is seek and follow him.

CAESAREA—CONCRETE PORT CITY

When Herod the Great went looking for a new harbor where ships sailing the Mediterranean Sea could be loaded and unloaded, he had a problem. There's barely a dent in the coast of Israel, not even a tiny bay to protect ships from the waves of the sea. It would be pretty hard to unload a rocking ship! But Herod figured his that Roman engineers would just love a challenge.

Rome conquered the world because they had a powerful army. But they also conquered the world because they were smart and had lots of brilliant technology—like concrete. Concrete was one of Rome's greatest inventions. Some of their concrete buildings have lasted 2,000 years! It was strong, easy to make, easy to form into all kinds of cool shapes, fireproof, and made building wa-a-ay faster than using stone!

So, Herod built up the town of Caesarea (named after Caesar) and put his engineers into overdrive building something very outstanding. They constructed one of the most

amazing structures of the ancient world—a huge, artificial harbor!

ROMAN SECRET FORMULA

First, Herod's Roman engineers used special hydraulic (underwater) concrete. It was a concrete mixture that could actually harden while under salt water! To do this neato trick, they added a pinch of volcanic ash from Rome.

Then they sank 50-foot stone and concrete blocks into the ocean. Wood frames around the blocks trapped ocean sand to add strength to the structure. Then a layer of rubble, and more concrete, created a wave-busting seawalls.

When the entire port was enclosed by the seawalls, it was an impressive 100-acre harbor!

Stone buildings and towers were then built on top of the seawalls.

All this took fewer than ten years to build!

Scuba diving archaeologists at Caesarea have found the ruins of harbor buildings on the sea bottom. Perhaps they were destroyed by earthquakes.

GET SMARTER

Just because something has been done one way for hundreds or thousands of years doesn't mean there's not a better way of doing things. The great inventors of the world have come up with amazing inventions. When you are stuck with a problem, learn to think like an inventor. Whether you're doing your chores or trying to solve a problem or get something done more quickly, pray to the God who created everything. He will show you a better, smarter way of doing things.

THE MASADA FORTRESS

Herod the Great built one of the world's most amazing palace-fortress-combination-super-structures in the entire ancient world. It was Masada. Masada was a natural fortress!

MASADA MASTERY

- The palace fortress of Masada was built on a 1,500-foot-high, flat-topped mountain.
- Masada was surrounded by miles of harsh desert and steep paths—one was and still is called Snake Path.
- Masada covered 23 acres of land on top of the mountain.
- Around the fort, Herod built a wall 4,250 feet long.
- Near the edge of the cliff, Herod built a three-level, luxury palace.
- The guy even had hot and cold baths, a swimming pool, a throne room, and three other palaces up there.
- The mountaintop also had barracks for soldiers and storage for an almost endless supply of food and water. They could even grow crops up there!

To get an idea of the size of mighty Masada, climb to the top of Devil's Tower, Wyoming. This volcanic cone soars 865 feet in the air and towers over the forest below, but it's still dwarfed by 1,500-foot-tall Masada.

Masada was unbeatable until the Romans decided to attack it almost 75 years after Herod built it. Jewish rebels were using Masada as a hideout, so the Roman commander Flavius Silva marched his soldiers and Jewish prisoners across the desert to Masada.

He placed army camps all around the mountain; then he had almost 15,000 Jewish prisoners build a six-foot-thick siege wall around the mountain.

He waited and waited. No surrender.

Next, he ordered tons of dirt and stone moved to the base of the mountain and built an earthen ramp right up the side of the mountain. After months of work, the ramp was an unbelievable 300 feet high and 600 feet long. The Romans built a large siege tower and battering ram and pushed them up the ramp. Even though the rebels threw down 100-pound rocks, they were no match for the Roman masters of disaster. The Romans took the fort.

GET COOLER

Being a go-getter is good. Getting things done, working hard, and being good at what you do is great. But life isn't just doing-it's also *being*. It is being a believer in God's son, Jesus. It's being a good person, a good friend, someday being a good father and husband. Herod was good at doing, but he died a disgusting, miserable death, and no one cared, because he never got the *being* part.

CORINTH

The apostle Paul must have looked around the wild seaport city of Corinth and prayed for strength. It was a big city with approximately 300,000 citizens plus 460,000 slaves. (Pssst, somebody should tell them that slaves are people, too!)

Corinth had a theater that could hold 18,000 people. Its temple for Apollo, the Greek god of the sun, was 174 feet long and 69 feet wide. Holding up the 24-foot-high roof were 38 big, stone columns.

Corinth was an extremely wealthy town, because it was in exactly the right spot. It had a booming and unusual business: The Corinthians hauled boats over dry land.

A Ship Highway

Sailing around the very tip of Greece (also called Cape Tenaron) with a ship full of cargo was a risky business. Sea captains often took their ships to the quiet waters of the Corinthian Gulf and then waited to sail over land! (No joke!)

- Small ships were hauled out of the water and loaded onto wagon trams.
- The ships were pulled over land on wagons for four miles to the calm waters of the Saronic Gulf on the other side.
- The ship and cargo were then launched back into the water.
- Bigger ships had their cargo unloaded, transported over land, and then reloaded onto different ships on the other side of the penninsula.

- This odd road-trip saved the captains almost 300 nautical miles of bad seas.
- Parts of the ancient, stone, tram road can still be seen today.

With all the temples and different idols being worshiped in Corinth, the apostle Paul found it tough to teach there. But that didn't stop him! Every Sabbath (without fail) he was at the synagogue, teaching about Jesus to both the Greeks and the Jews. And many people became believers because Paul was a no-stop kind of guy! (Acts 18:1–8).

GET SMARTER

How long does it take to boil a three-minute egg or watch a TV sitcom? Some things in life take a certain amount of time. Other things, like growing up or getting to know God or working through life's problems, are a little harder to estimate. The Corinthians found a major shortcut for their ships by using their heads. But for many of us, there are not shortcuts. We just have to be patient and trust God with our lives, because for some things there are no shortcuts. Praying for God's wisdom, using the brain God gave us, and working hard will usually be the quickest way to accomplish our goals.

ATHENS

Romans were known for their cruelty, their army, and their snobbish we-rule-the-world-and-we're-so-o-o-much-better-than-everybody-else attitude. The Greeks, however, were known for their smarts, their ideas about people making their own government (psst, that's democracy), and their love of art. But that didn't mean that the Greeks didn't also have fights and wars. They had plenty, and the big city of Athens had always been a well-fortified city.

By the time the apostle Paul visited Athens, it was a huge, busy, seaport city of around 200,000 people. The ancient city was actually sort of split into two sections. One section, the Agora, was a place full of markets, schools, and law courts. The other part was on a 500-foot hill called the Acropolis. Overlooking the city and ocean was a group of amazing marble buildings. The Parthenon Temple of Athena was the best and biggest building there. It was an amazing 65 feet high, 284 feet long, and 111 feet wide, and it had 600 sculpted figures on panels set all

around the building. Today, 2,400 years after the
Parthenon was built, thousands of visitors stare at the
columned shell of the great building. Inside, there was
once a huge statue of the goddess Athena, carved of
wood and covered in gold and ivory. Legend tells us
that enemies of the artist accused him of stealing
some of the gold from the statue. He said that he
hadn't stolen the gold, so he took all the gold off,
weighed it, and proved his innocence!

Athens was also home to a tall, enormous temple to
the Greek top-dog god, Zeus. When Paul visited the

temple of Zeus, it was a hard-hat zone—the temple was still under construction. This temple had fewer than 104 columns that were 56 feet high, which would make the temple an impressive 90 feet tall when the roof was added. That's like a nine-story building! This made the Zeus temple one of the largest buildings in the ancient world! It was 345 feet long and 135 feet wide. Now, just imagine the gold-and-ivory statue of Zeus that must have been in that building! Those Athenians sure liked their city, temples, and statues big and showy! But they didn't impress our guy, Paul.

GET SMARTER

In the busy public market (Agora) of Athens was the Bouleuterion, a clubhouse where the Areopagus (Mar's Hill) council met. Now, some of the Greek brain-heads (philosophers) heard Paul preaching and pulled him in front of their smartie-guy council. They called Paul a babbler or seed picker—meaning, he talked a lot but wasn't smart enough to actually be smart. Paul talked about all the temples in Athens, then told them that God didn't live in a temple! God was everywhere and knew everything all the time. He so impressed some of the brain-heads that they became believers. When God's with you, you have access to his smarts.

ALEXANDRIA —IS GREAT!

A world-conquering, kingdom-tromping, young Greek general named Alexander the Great built a new Greek-style city in the lower Nile delta in Egypt. Approximately 300,000 Greeks, Egyptians, and Jews lived there. Many Jews from Israel even returned to Egypt and settled in Alexandria. It soon became a hot spot for deep thinkers and ancient scientists, so an Egyptian pharaoh named Ptolemy I built a super-deluxe library in Alexandria.

CHECKOUT TIME AT THE LIBRARY

- There were from 400,000 to 900,000 papyrus scrolls and books there.
- The librarians tried to collect every book or scroll in the ancient world.
- Legend says that, by law, every ship that left the city had to be searched for stolen scrolls.

Over time, the library was destroyed and became another unsolved mystery in the pages of history.

But Alexandria was also home to one of The Seven Wonders of the Ancient World—a gigantic lighthouse on the island of Pharos.

LIGHTHOUSE LEGENDS

The Pharos lighthouse was built like a modern sky-scraper, with an awesome 384 feet of towering marble. That's taller than a 30-story building! Even the Statue of Liberty in New York harbor, at 305 feet, can't beat this monster building!

- On top of the lighthouse was a statue of the Greek god Poseidon.

- Inside was a spiral ramp that allowed horse-drawn carts to take stuff up to the top.

- A large mirror (probably of polished metal) reflected sunlight during the day. A large fire was lit at night.

- Legend says that the lighthouse could be seen from as far away as 100 miles.

- Stories were told of a treasure hidden under the lighthouse.

- One wild story said that the lighthouse could create a beam of light that would find and destroy enemy ships. (They wished!)

- Another tall tale was that the lighthouse could spy on cities far across the sea by reflecting their image onto the great mirror.
- The lighthouse stood for about 1,500 years before being toppled by two strong earthquakes.
- Archeologists are still working hard to uncover the true facts about the great and mysterious lighthouse of Egypt.

GET SMARTER

Legends start when someone tells a story they're not too sure about—or they're just guessing—but they tell it to others as if it were a fact. We know that some of the legends about the Alexandria lighthouse were made up, because they're just not possible. A man of God protects the truth and his reputation as a truth-teller. How do you do that?

(1) Never lie.
(2) If you're not sure of the facts or you're guessing, always say so.
(3) If you're telling a joke or just making up a story for fun, come clean at the end and make sure everyone knows that.

EPHESUS

The ancient seaport city of Ephesus was another Roman command post. Makes you think Romans ruled the world or something. Ephesus had about 225,000 people living there, which might explain why they had one of the largest ancient amphitheaters in the world.

SHOWTIME IN EPHESUS

- The outdoor theater held a no-elbow-room crowd of 25,000 to 50,000 people! Hope everybody had a bath!
- It had 12 stairways that led down to an 80-foot-long, 20-foot-deep stage.

Now, if theater was a little boring or too bloody, you could check out one of The Seven Wonders of the Ancient World, located right in Ephesus. The amazing and totally 100-percent marble temple of the goddess, Artemis!

HUNTING FOR TEMPLE FACTS

- The temple of Artemis was 180 feet wide and 377 feet long and was at least 60 feet tall.
- It had about 120 columns that were about

six feet around. Some were even covered in gold!
Bet those were guarded.

- Inside the temple were bronze statues of warrior
  women called Amazons, and probably a statue of
  the goddess herself.
- Archaeologists have uncovered ancient gifts that
  people left for the goddess: gold, silver, or ivory
  goddess statues, earrings, bracelets, and necklaces.
  Girlie stuff!
- The temple may have been used as a bank for kings
  and rich people.

When the apostle Paul was in Ephesus, he led many
Ephesians to Jesus. These new believers stopped
going to the temple of Artemis, and this got the statue

makers really uptight. If this kept up, they'd be out of a job! A huge, angry mob grabbed some of Paul's friends and dragged them to the theater. For two hours they stood around the theater, shouting, "Great is Artemis of the Ephesians!" (see Acts 19:23–41).

Time surely changes things—about 200 years later some tough guys named the Goths attacked many of cities along the Mediterranean Sea, including Ephesus. The place never really recovered. The harbor filled in and soon the entire city was abandoned. But in 1863 archaeologists started to uncover the past glory that was Ephesus. Yee-haw! Another dirt-old city to dig around in!

GET DEEPER

Some women get offended that we call God "him." They feel that's part of the problem of men's thinking that they rule and women drool. Some guys do have a problem with "superiority over women" attitudes, and that's not right. God doesn't favor men over women. Men aren't better than women. We're all his children and equally as special, gifted, and loved. The only reason we call God "he" and "Father" is because that's what he calls himself in his book, the Bible.

THE CITY OF ROME

There is a myth that long ago two little kids named Romulus and Remus were lost but got found by a she-wolf. She raised them as her own pups (kind of like Mowgli). Later, when the guys grew up, they built the city of Rome. And that's how the Romans explained the start of their city. Really, Rome started when people moved into the area and liked it. Rome grew bigger and fought with neighbors until it slowly grew tough and powerful. Eventually, Rome took over the world!

The city of Rome became the royal city for the Roman king (Caesar). The rich and powerful city of Rome was the center of the ancient world. It had around 1.2 million people living there, and at one point there were more slaves than Romans. (Rome was about the size of a modern-day city like Dallas, Texas.) Roman slaves came from all over the conquered world. Maybe that's why people say, "All roads lead to Rome." Romans put their engineers to use building roads to the most remote outposts of their huge empire.

Roman Roadways

When Romans built a new roadway, first, the area was mapped; then the soil was plowed to loosen it, the ground was dug down, the dirt was stamped down firmly, then sand and stones were put down; concrete was poured, and last, stone blocks were laid on top.

- The Romans built more than 50,000 miles of high way and 200,000 miles of smaller roads-enough road to go around the world ten times.
- Each mile of road was marked by a pillar, which gave the distance from Rome. ("Are we there yet?")
- The roads had a system of rest areas and military forts along the way.
- The average Roman road traveler could cover 25 miles a day.

Running Water

Romans also designed a totally mind-boggling system of above- and below-ground man-made channels to get water into their cities. These aqueducts took water from its source and carried it in gently sloping waterways downhill to the city.

- The Romans spent 500 years building 11 super aqueducts into the growing city of Rome.
- The longest aqueduct is 57 miles long.

Engineers began to build totally cool arched bridges. Some were 100 feet high with double or triple levels of supporting archways. Compare that with the London Bridge, built in 1821 out of granite. It had five arches and was 928 feet long and 49 feet wide. Romans still ruled when it came to building great stuff.

The Romans even designed special, slow pools that trapped junk so that the water stayed clean.

When the water reached Rome, wealthy homeowners could pay to have water channeled to their properties. But, for the most part, the water went to public fountains where ordinary citizens carried it home in vases.

Some of the Roman aqueducts are still in use today! Built to last!

Forget emperors, generals, and armies! Hats off to the determined Roman engineers and builders who clearly showed the world they were the real master builders and empire makers in Rome!

COLISEUM— THEATER OF DEATH

The Romans had a reputation for being bloodthirsty and nasty! Imagine 50,000 people gathered in a huge theater just to watch people kill each other in strange and gross ways. It took ten years to build the place where a lot of this happened—the Coliseum. It was a huge, 160-foot-tall outdoor theater with four, separate floors and 80 entrances. Just like today, spectators had

numbered tickets with matching seats. A 15-foot-high wall separated the audience from the fighters or gladiators, below. The action took place on the arena's sand-covered, removable wood floor. Under the arena

was a basement full of rooms and cages. Animals and fighters were brought up to the arena through a series of ramps, stairways, and even ancient elevators. The crowds came for one purpose—to see a bloody show!

• These were battles to the death! Hundreds of gladiators might fight in just one event. Sometimes animals were forced to fight each other, such as a bull fighting a rhinoceros.

• Over 10,000 people met their deaths in the arena.

• Church history tells us thousands of Christians were killed by lions in the Coliseum and in other Roman arenas across the empire.

• Ancient records report 5,000 animals killed in a single day: lions, tigers, buffaloes, elephants, hippopotamuses, rhinoceroses, bulls, horses, boars, and bears. (Guess they were keeping track so they could order more!)

• The wooden arena floor could be removed and the lower basement flooded for mock sea battles. Adding man-eating crocodiles, gave a realistic touch.

• Archers were set high above to shoot animals that threatened to escape into the audience. Although . . . protecting the audience wasn't that important! One emperor, having run out of gladiators, picked a section of the audience and used them in the games! Nice guy.

- Gladiators were trained slaves, prisoners of war, and sometimes criminals. It also became extremely trendy for young Romans to volunteer. Some popular gladiators were like (ancient) rock stars. And a slave could earn his freedom by becoming a popular gladiator, but if you were a bad fighter, the crowd would yell to have your throat cut.

Finally, after the empire became Christian, the bloody games were outlawed. The Coliseum was later damaged by several earthquakes. If you ever go to Rome, you'll see that the Coliseum is still standing—most of it, anyway.

GET STRONGER

What do you suppose God thinks about fighting and bullying? There's nothing wrong with competition and testing our physical abilities against each other. But when we want to hurt someone or use fighting to "get" someone or "get even," we've crossed the line. God wants us to respect one another and settle our differences in peaceful ways.

LABYRINTH OF THE DEAD

The dark, narrow passage is only three-to-four feet wide, and the darkness past the torchlight seems to go on forever. The tunnel twists, turns, and follows rough stairways deeper and deeper into the earth. On either side, dug into the earthen walls, are the burial chambers of ancient Christians. Sometimes the bones of three or more people lie in each tiny chamber. These are the catacombs of Rome—miles and miles of underground cemeteries.

Early Christians living in ancient Rome met secretly deep underground. But how did this all start? Christians didn't like to cremate (burn) the bodies of their dead as the Romans did. They wanted to bury them. Christians got land outside the city of Rome and dug out burial tunnels. Small coffin-sized burial chambers were cut into the walls. Over the years, gravediggers called *fossores* dug out miles of passages, graves, stairs, and sometimes even small, underground rooms for family-sized crypts. Some areas have four or five levels of underground passages.

Family and friends would write on the grave slabs, just as families inscribe tombstones today. Often, Christian symbols could be found, such as the dove, palm branch, olive branch, or an anchor. Sometimes gifts were left at the tomb.

CATACOMB FACTS

- There are 600 miles of catacombs around Rome.
- During the 200s and 300s, persecuted Christians cut 360 of those catacomb miles.
- In some places there are five levels of catacombs, some 65 feet down.
- Small chapel rooms (large enough for 50 people) were added to the tunnels.
- Some entrances to the catacombs had missing stairs, so a ladder was needed to get inside. Perhaps as a safety feature to keep out unwanted visitors.
- The catacombs are an amazing, if not kind of spooky, walk into Christian history!

New Jerusalem— Whole New Place

Until now we've been digging in the past, but now it's time to go to the future and explore the most amazing city ever! Chapters 21–22 of the Book of Revelation, tell us that God has built a new city of Jerusalem in heaven just for us. The apostle John saw a totally awesome city actually coming down from heaven and in that extremely cool city, God would live with his people forever. No one really knows if this city is literal or symbolic because Revelation 21:9-10 says that New Jerusalem is the Church. But just the same, check out the incredible dimensions God gave for this city—it beats anything ever made on this planet!

- The city is 1,400 miles long, wide, and tall! There has never, ever been anything that big!
- The wall around the city is 200 feet thick and completely made of jasper, a shiny, crystal-like stone.

- There are 12 gates all around the city, with an angel standing by each one! Each "always open" gate is made of (get this) one very large pearl. (You have to wonder where those monster oysters are living.)
- The city inside is made of pure gold—including the streets! And the entire city glows like a jewel in the way that a diamond sparkles!
- In fact, New Jerusalem is built with and decorated with jewels of every kind!
- The city doesn't need the sun or moon for light, because God's glory is going to shine the place up!
- Jesus told us that God has prepared a special home (a mansion) for each of us there (John 14:1–3). And because God loves us completely, you know that your room will be awesome!

The most important thing to remember is that only the people who believe in Jesus and who have their names written in God's book get to go inside God's city.

GET DEEPER

The people whom we read about in the Bible lived in amazing times and saw some awesome sights, but all of them were looking forward to something way better. The Bible says that Abraham was looking forward to a city that wasn't here but in heaven (Hebrews 11:10, 16). Today the world is full of great buildings and wonderful things to see, and in its own way, this is an incredible time to be alive. But it's still nothing, compared with what God has waiting for us. Not even close! When we become Christians, we become citizens of heaven. (We're actually just visitors down here.) Jesus died and paid the penalty for sin so we could spend all of eternity with God, away from the sins that have destroyed people's lives since Adam and Eve. We'll be able to enjoy all of heaven and the awesomeness of God and his building abilities forever. If you haven't become a citizen of heaven yet, you can pray this prayer, accept what Jesus did for you, and reserve your mansion in heaven:

Dear God, I know I've done bad and selfish things. I'm sorry. Please forgive me. I know that your Son, Jesus, died for me and was raised from the dead. I believe in him. Please make me your child. Please help me to love and obey you and learn more about you. In Jesus' name. Amen.

If you prayed this prayer sincerely, you are now God's child!

Conclusion

Many of the ancient cities mentioned in the Bible still have puzzling mysteries surrounding them. There are many unanswered questions. Is the golden ark of the covenant hidden somewhere under Jerusalem or in Ethiopia, as the Ethiopians claim? What still lies buried beneath sand in the treasure cities of Pharaoh? Some answers are just waiting to be discovered—some by accident, and some by researchers who have worked hard to solve ancient riddles.

Ancient exploration is one way by which Christians can better understand the people in the Bible. Digging through the past is like taking a time machine to another time and seeing the world through ancient eyes. How did Joseph feel when he first saw the pyramids? How did the apostle Paul feel when he walked through Athens two thousand years ago?

When we put ourselves in the ancient shoes of Bible people, we suddenly see that we're not that different from them after all! Someday, maybe, you'll stand in the ruins of some ancient city and follow the dusty footsteps of the heroes in the Bible. And suddenly . . . thousands of years won't seem that long ago after all.

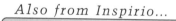

We want to hear from you. Please send your comments about this book to us in care of the address below. Thank you.

Zonderkidz®

Grand Rapids, MI 49530
www.zonderkidz.com